This book belongs to

_____

_____

for
Willem
J.C.

First published in Great Britain in 2008
This paperback edition published in 2009 by

Gullane Children's Books

185 Fleet Street, London, EC4A 2HS
www.gullanebooks.com

1   3   5   7   9   10   8   6   4   2

Illustrations © Jane Cabrera 2008

The right of Jane Cabrera to be identified as the author
and illustrator of this work has been asserted by her in
accordance with the copyright, Designs and Patents Act, 1988.
A CIP record for this title is available from the British Library.

ISBN: 978-1-86233-750-3

Printed and bound in Indonesia

OLD MACDONALD
had a FARM

Jane
Cabrera

GULLANE
CHILDREN'S BOOKS

Old MacDonald
had a farm,
ee-i-ee-i-o.

And on his farm he had a wife,
ee-i-ee-i-o.
With a **kiss kiss** here,
and a **kiss kiss** there,
here a **kiss**, there a **kiss**,
everywhere a
kiss kiss.

Old MacDonald had a wife, **ee-i-ee-i-o**.

Old MacDonald had a farm, **ee-i-ee-i-o**.
And on his farm he had a dog, **ee-i-ee-i-o**.
With a **woof woof** here, and a **woof woof**
there, here a **woof**, there a **woof**,
everywhere a **woof woof**.

Old MacDonald
had a dog,
ee-i-ee-i-o.

Old MacDonald had a farm, **ee-i-ee-i-o**.
And on his farm he had some sheep, **ee-i-ee-i-o**.
With a **baa baa** here, and a **baa baa** there,
here a **baa**, there a **baa**,
everywhere a **baa baa**.

Old MacDonald
had some sheep,
ee-i-ee-i-o.

Old MacDonald had a farm, **ee-i-ee-i-o**.
And on his farm he had a horse, **ee-i-ee-i-o**.
With a **neigh neigh** here, and a **neigh neigh** there,
here a **neigh**, there a **neigh**,
everywhere a **neigh neigh**.

Old MacDonald
had a horse,
ee-i-ee-i-o.

Old MacDonald had a farm, **ee-i-ee-i-o**.
And on his farm he had some hens, **ee-i-ee-i-o**.
With a **cluck cluck** here, and a **cluck cluck** there,
here a **cluck**, there a **cluck**,
everywhere a **cluck cluck**.

Old MacDonald
had some hens,
ee-i-ee-i-o.

Old MacDonald had a farm, **ee-i-ee-i-o**.
And on his farm he had a goat, **ee-i-ee-i-o**.
With a **munch munch** here, and a **munch munch** there,
here a **munch**, there a **munch**,
everywhere a **munch munch**.

Old MacDonald
had a goat,
ee-i-ee-i-o.

Old MacDonald had a farm, **ee-i-ee-i-o**.
And on his farm he had some ducks, **ee-i-ee-i-o**.
With a **quack quack** here, and a **quack quack** there,
here a **quack**, there a **quack**,
everywhere a **quack quack**.

Old MacDonald
had some ducks,
ee-i-ee-i-o.

Old MacDonald had a farm, **ee-i-ee-i-o**.
And on his farm he had a cow, **ee-i-ee-i-o**.
With a **moo moo** here, and a **moo moo** there,
here a **moo**, there a **moo**,
everywhere a **moo moo**.

Old MacDonald
had a cow,
ee-i-ee-i-o.

Old MacDonald had a farm, **ee-i-ee-i-o**.
And on his farm he had a pig, **ee-i-ee-i-o**.
With an **oink oink** here, and an **oink oink** there,
here an **oink**, there an **oink**,
everywhere an **oink oink**.

Old MacDonald had a pig, **ee-i-ee-i-o**.

Old MacDonald had a farm, **ee-i-ee-i-o**.
And on his farm he heard all this, **ee-i-ee-i-o**.

Woof Woof,
Baa Baa,
Neigh Neigh,
Cluck Cluck
Munch Munch,
Quack Quack,
Moo Moo,
Oink Oink.

Waa! Waa!
...?

Old MacDonald had a...

BABY!
Ee-i-ee-i-o!